A River Leaks Through It

Owlkids Books

Chirp, Tweet, and Squawk loved to play in their playhouse. On this particular day, they were playing…

"Explorers!" said Squawk.

"Explorers paddling down a mighty river!" said Tweet.

"Explorers paddling down a mighty river in search of the world's biggest waterfall!" said Chirp.

"Whoa! What's happening?" asked Squawk, as their boat rocked.

"We've hit some rapids!" said Tweet.

"What are rapids?" asked Squawk.

"Rapids are the fast-moving parts of a river," said Chirp.

"Can't they be less rapid?" asked Squawk.

Soon, explorers Chirp, Tweet, and Squawk were spinning in circles!

"Look out for the rocks!" yelled Squawk.

"Paddle right!" yelled Chirp.

"Paddle left!" yelled Squawk.

"Stop paddling in my face!" yelled Tweet.

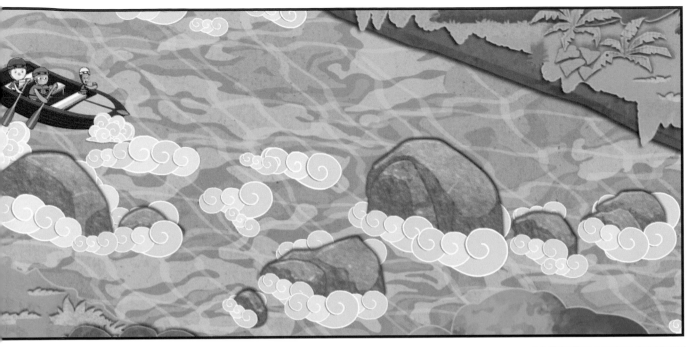

Suddenly, the boat struck a sharp rock!

"Hey," said Squawk. "Why are my feet wet?"

"The boat has sprung a leak!" said Tweet.

"Oh, no!" said Chirp. "We need something to plug the hole!"

"Look in our dry pack!" said Tweet.

"What's a dry pack?" asked Squawk.

"It's a waterproof bag to keep your things in when you're boating," said Tweet.

"Right," said Chirp. "Look in the box—I mean, dry pack—with all the helpful stuff in it."

The three explorers opened the lid and looked inside.

"I see lots of popsicle sticks, tinfoil, and toothpicks," said Tweet.

"Oh, look!" said Chirp. "There are some corks in here, too!"

"What's a cork?" asked Squawk.

"Corks are made from the bark of the cork oak tree," said Chirp. "They float and can be used to plug bottles of water and other liquids."

"Plug bottles of water, huh?" said Tweet.

Explorers Chirp, Tweet, and Squawk rushed back to their boat.

"Help me use the cork to plug the leak!" said Chirp.

"Hurry! Now my knees are wet!" said Squawk.

"There!" said Tweet. "Our watery woes are over!"

The explorers then continued their search for the world's biggest waterfall...

"Do you guys hear that?" asked Chirp.

"It sounds like someone taking a shower," said Squawk. "A hundred showers!"

"That's the sound of a waterfall!" said Tweet. "We must be really close."

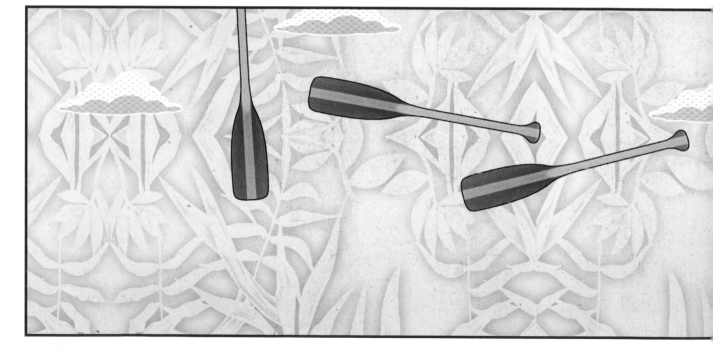

Actually, explorers Chirp, Tweet, and Squawk were *too* close to the world's biggest waterfall...

"Ahh!" yelled Tweet. "We're falling!"

"Ahh!" yelled Squawk. "We're...still...falling!"

"Ahh!" yelled Chirp. "I told you, it's the world's biggest waterfall!"

"Then we have time to make a plan before our boat crashes at the bottom!" said Tweet.

"Do we have time to build a helicopter?" asked Squawk.

"No," said Chirp. "But we can float on our corks!"

The boat crashed at the bottom of the world's biggest waterfall, but Chirp, Tweet, and Squawk jumped out just in time and used their corks to float to safety.

"It worked!" said Tweet.

"These corks are just like little boats!" said Chirp.

"Row, row, row your cork," sang Squawk. "How I love my cork...!"

"That was fun, you guys!" said Chirp.

"Let's do that again!" said Tweet.

"Only this time," said Squawk, "let's surf down the world's biggest waterfall!"

From an episode of the animated TV series *Chirp*, produced by Sinking Ship (Chirp) Productions. Based on the Chirp character created by Bob Kain.

Based on the TV episode *A River Leaks Through It* written by Sheila Dinsmore. Story adaptation written by J. Torres.

CHIRP and the CHIRP character are trademarks of Bayard Presse Canada Inc.

Text © 2015 Owlkids Books Inc.
Interior illustrations by Smiley Guy Studios. © 2015 Sinking Ship (Chirp) Productions. Used under license.
Cover illustration by Cale Atkinson, based on images from the TV episode. Cover illustration © 2015 Owlkids Books Inc.

Owlkids Books acknowledges the financial support of the Canada Council for the Arts, the Ontario Arts Council, the Government of Canada through the Canada Book Fund (CBF) and the Government of Ontario through the Ontario Media Development Corporation's Book Initiative for our publishing activities.

Published in Canada by
Owlkids Books Inc.
10 Lower Spadina Avenue
Toronto, ON M5V 2Z2

Library and Archives Canada Cataloguing in Publication

Torres, J., 1969-, author
     A river leaks through it / adapted by J. Torres.

(Chirp ; 7) Based on the TV program Chirp; writer of the episode, A river leaks through it, Sheila Dinsmore.

ISBN 978-1-77147-181-7 (pbk.).--ISBN 978-1-77147-182-4 (bound)

     I. Dinsmore, Sheila, author II. Title.

PS8589.O6755667R59 2015   jC813'.54   C2015-903659-3

Edited by: Jennifer Stokes
Designed by: Susan Sinclair

Funded by the Government of Canada
Financé par le gouvernement du Canada

Manufactured in Altona, MB, Canada, in July 2015, by Friesens Corporation
Job #213923

A   B   C   D   E   F

Publisher of Chirp, chickaDEE and OWL
www.owlkidsbooks.com

Owlkids Books is a division of Bayard CANADA